WORLDWIDE ADVENTURES 6

The African Safari
Discovery

CATCH FLAT STANLEY'S
WORLDWIDE ADVENTURES:

The Mount Rushmore Calamity

The Great Egyptian Grave Robbery

The Japanese Ninja Surprise

The Intrepid Canadian Expedition

The Amazing Mexican Secret

The African Safari Discovery

AND DON'T MISS ANY OF THESE
OUTRAGEOUS STORIES:

Flat Stanley: His Original Adventure!

Stanley and the Magic Lamp

Invisible Stanley

Stanley's Christmas Adventure

Stanley in Space

Stanley, Flat Again!

FLAT STANLEY's
WORLDWIDE ADVENTURES
BOOK No. 6

The African Safari
Discovery

CREATED BY **Jeff Brown**
WRITTEN BY **Josh Greenhut**
PICTURES BY **Macky Pamintuan**

HARPER
An Imprint of HarperCollinsPublishers

Library of Congress Cataloging-in-Publication Data
Greenhut, Josh.
  The African safari discovery / created by Jeff Brown ; written by Josh Greenhut ;
pictures by Macky Pamintuan. — 1st ed.
    p. cm. — (Flat Stanley's worldwide adventures ; 6)
  Summary: Flat Stanley, his father, and his brother travel to Africa in search of a
recently discovered flat skull, hoping it will provide clues to Stanley's condition.
  ISBN 978-0-06-143001-5 (trade bdg.) — ISBN 978-0-06-143000-8 (pbk. bdg.)
  [1. Voyages and travels—Fiction. 2. Adventure and adventurers—Fiction.
3. Africa—Fiction.] I. Brown, Jeff, 1926–2003. II. Pamintuan, Macky, ill. III. Title.
PZ7.G84568Af 2011   2010022978
[Fic]—dc22   CIP
                                                                          AC
Typography by Alison Klapthor
                16 17 18 19 20 OPM 10
❖
First Edition

CONTENTS

The African Safari
Discovery

1

The Search Begins

Stanley Lambchop was flattened against the wall outside the kitchen. He knew it was impolite to eavesdrop, but his mother sounded upset. And she was talking about *him*.

"I'm worried about Stanley," Harriet Lambchop was saying to her husband, George. "What if he's flat for the rest of his life? You know how difficult things can be for someone who's special."

Stanley thought of the morning, not long ago, when he awoke to find that the bulletin board over his bed had fallen on him during the night. Ever since, he'd been only half an inch thick. With his new shape, Stanley could do all sorts of things most people couldn't do, such as travel via airmail. But his mother was right. Just yesterday, someone at school had called him "Boardbrains."

"I'm sure everything will be fine, dear," Mr. Lambchop said. "Just because Stanley has gone flat—"

"*Become* flat," Mrs. Lambchop said. "Stanley hasn't *gone* flat, George. He's *become* flat. You know how improper grammar makes me—" She was overcome with emotion.

Stanley peeled himself off the wall and trudged down the hall. He felt like being alone.

A moment later, he was flat on his back beneath the couch in the living room. It may have been too low to the ground for the vacuum cleaner, but it wasn't too low for Stanley . . . or for how he felt.

Stanley should have been excited to find all the things that he and his little brother, Arthur, had lost under the couch. There was a dusty origami ninja star, which Stanley had made after traveling by mail to meet the boys' idol, the martial arts star Oda Nobu, in Japan. There was a hockey puck from a professional game in Canada where Stanley had recently slid across the ice. There was a yellow race car that Arthur liked to run down Stanley's body like a giant ramp.

Stanley didn't want to be flat forever. He imagined how lonely he would be if he were the only flat person he knew for as long as he lived.

The doorbell rang. Stanley heard his father answer it.

"Mr. Dart!" Mr. Lambchop said.

Mr. O. Jay Dart was the director of the Famous Museum and the Lambchops' neighbor. Stanley had helped him foil some sneak thieves when he first became flattened. He'd had to dress up like a shepherdess in a white dress and a curly wig and pretend to be in a painting. It was humiliating.

"Good morning, George. Have you seen this morning's paper?" Mr. Dart said as Mr. Lambchop led him into the kitchen.

A minute later, Stanley's father called, "Stanley!"

Oh, great, thought Stanley. I must be in trouble.

"Stanley?" his father shouted again.

Stanley saw Arthur's sneakers race into the living room. "Stanley! Stanley!"

"Stanley?" Mrs. Lambchop's gray high-heeled shoes marched past.

"Stanley! Stanley? Stanley! *Stanley!*" Shoes paraded before Stanley's eyes. Doors opened and closed in other rooms. His family and Mr. Dart were looking everywhere for him.

"Where could that boy be?" Mrs. Lambchop returned to the living room, her toe tapping the carpet anxiously.

"You're sure he didn't go out?" Mr. Dart's brown loafers asked.

"Maybe he saw it already," wondered Arthur's sneakers.

Stanley slid his head out from under

the couch and looked up at everyone towering over him. "Saw what?"

Mr. Dart thrust the newspaper in Stanley's face. "Stanley, my boy, they found a flat skull in Africa!"

Stanley read.

FLAT SKULL DISCOVERED IN AFRICA

Scientists claimed to make a startling discovery yesterday when they unearthed a flat skull in remote Tanzania. The skull is highly unusual due to its shape. Scientists believe that this may be the missing link between flat creatures and regular ones. The discovery was nearly lost forever after a group of local children tried to play a game similar to "Frisbee" with it.

Everyone took a seat around the kitchen table.

"I hereby call this special session of the Lambchop family meeting to order," announced Mr. Lambchop.

"Let's begin by welcoming our esteemed guest," said Mrs. Lambchop. "Mr. Dart, would you like a snack?" She slid a bowl across the table. It was filled with chips sprinkled with the secret ingredient that Stanley had recently retrieved from Mexico.

Stanley stared at his hands. He was thinking that he should go to Africa to see the flat skull. Maybe he wasn't so alone after all.

"I want to get mailed to Africa," he declared.

"Absolutely not," said Mrs. Lambchop. "It's one thing to fly airmail to a major city like Tokyo, Cairo, or Mexico City. Who knows how often mail is delivered in the most remote regions of Africa?"

"Your mother is right, Stanley," said Mr. Lambchop. "It isn't safe."

"But I have to! What if that skull is the same as me?"

Mr. and Mrs. Lambchop exchanged looks.

"No way," Arthur blurted, as if reading their minds. "I am NOT missing another big adventure. Stanley gets to circle the globe, while I have to stay home and miss all the fun. It isn't fair!"

"These are the most delicious chips I've ever tasted!" said Mr. Dart, shoveling another handful into his mouth.

"Maybe we should all go," Mr. Lambchop suggested.

"I can't, George," said Mrs. Lambchop. "I'm hosting my fund-raiser for the Grammar Society on Saturday. I still have to dot the *i*'s and cross the *t*'s on all of the place cards. Besides, how could we possibly afford airplane tickets to Africa?"

"Perhaps you could fly courtesy of the Famous Museum," said Mr. Dart. "After all, investigating a major archaeological find would qualify as official museum business. It's the least we could do for you, Stanley, after all your help.

"Of course, we could justify only two airplane tickets to our board of directors," added Mr. Dart.

Arthur groaned. "That figures."

"I could stay folded in the pocket on the back of the airplane seat," Stanley offered, "so both you and Dad could come."

"You would do that?" said Arthur.

"Sure," said Stanley. "I'd only slip out

from under the seat belt anyway."

"That settles it," decided Mr. Lambchop. "Boys, pack your bags for Africa!"

2

Nairobi

Since becoming flat, Stanley had grown used to traveling long distances in small spaces. But the flight to Nairobi, the capital of Kenya, was particularly difficult. The flight attendant had insisted that Stanley could not be folded into a seat pocket—"That boy is nearly the size of a small sleeping bag, sir," she had said. "It's unsafe." Despite Mr.

Lambchop's protests, she demanded that Stanley be checked underneath the cabin with the passenger baggage.

As a result, Stanley had spent the entire flight in the noisy belly of the airplane, with no one to talk to except a very frightened caged poodle, a set of golf clubs, and many large suitcases. Stanley had a great deal of time during his trip to ponder how hard a life of flatness could be.

Needless to say, he was very relieved when the rubber flaps on the baggage conveyor belt brushed his forehead, and he emerged into the bright light of the airport.

"There he is!" cried Arthur. Mr.

Lambchop ran up and pulled Stanley off the baggage carousel. It felt awfully good to stretch out.

The moment they stepped outside, the three Lambchops were surrounded by people offering to take them wherever they wanted to go.

Mr. Lambchop pursed his lips and peered around, looking lost. This made people shout more loudly. Someone yelling, "You need a taxi!" almost knocked Stanley over like a piece of cardboard.

"Stanley, where's your brother?" Mr. Lambchop asked suddenly in a panicked voice. Stanley glanced around and saw nothing but a sea of arms waving in his face. "Lift me up," he said, and Mr. Lambchop raised him over the crowd like a periscope. Stanley saw Arthur making his way through the crowd, followed by an African boy about Arthur's age.

"Here he is," said Stanley matter-of-factly.

"Arthur Lambchop," scolded Mr. Lambchop, "how dare you wander off

in a strange country!"

"But this boy can help us," said Arthur. "His name is Odinga."

Odinga smiled brightly at Stanley.

"Hello," said Stanley and Mr. Lambchop.

Odinga said nothing.

"He doesn't speak English," explained Arthur.

"Arthur," said Mr. Lambchop, "what have I told you about going off with strangers?"

"But I *know* we can trust Odinga," said Arthur.

"How?" Mr. Lambchop crossed his arms.

Arthur pointed to Odinga's T-shirt.

The picture on it was very faded, and Stanley had to lean closer to see. He was surprised to find a picture of himself in a ninja outfit flying through the air with his leg thrust outward. It had been taken when he was in Japan, and briefly associated with the movie business.

Odinga gave Stanley two very enthusiastic thumbs-up.

Stanley felt his cheeks turn red. It must be the Kenyan heat.

"Show him the newspaper, Dad," prodded Arthur.

Mr. Lambchop reached into his pocket and unfolded the article he had clipped two days before. He held it out to Odinga, pointing to the map with the X on it, which marked the place where the flat skull had been discovered.

Odinga looked at the piece of paper, turned on his heel, and walked away.

Mr. Lambchop raised his eyebrows at Arthur as if to say, "I told you so." Then Odinga reappeared and grabbed Arthur's arm. He wanted the Lambchops to follow him.

Walking quickly, Odinga led them through the crowd to an old minivan waiting by the curb. It was already full of people. Standing beside it was a girl who looked not much older than Stanley. Odinga went up to her and said something in Swahili. She approached the Lambchops.

"I am Bisa," she said in heavily accented English. "My brother tells me you need to go to Tanzania."

Once again, Mr. Lambchop held out the newspaper clipping.

"Why do you want to go there?" Bisa asked. "It is very far."

Stanley stepped forward. He turned sideways to show how flat he was. Then he turned to face her again. "I'm looking for answers," he said simply.

Bisa said, "What if you do not like the answers you find?"

Stanley could only shrug.

"I understand," she said quietly. "Come," she declared with sudden excitement. "My father will help you. He is a good pilot."

As the minibus bounced through the streets of Nairobi, Stanley's entire face was pressed against the window. This was because so many people were squeezed into the minibus with him. Apart from Arthur, Mr. Lambchop, Odinga, and Bisa, passengers were constantly jumping on and off.

Nairobi was a big city. Bisa said

that three million people lived there. Everywhere, the streets were teeming with traffic. They passed open-air markets filled with fruits and vegetables of every color. People were cooking on the side of the road. Skyscrapers towered over the city.

"Look, Arthur!" Stanley said, elbowing his brother as they passed a man with a giant bird on his shoulder.

Arthur squeezed his face beside Stanley's.

Finally, Bisa and Odinga jumped out of the open door of the minivan, and the Lambchops rushed to follow. Bisa waved for them to hurry up as she climbed the steps of a building.

Mr. Lambchop grabbed Stanley and Arthur's arms suddenly. He pointed to a sign next to the door: NAIROBI POLICE DEPARTMENT.

"It's a setup!" Mr. Lambchop gulped.

Stanley and Arthur looked at each other.

"What is wrong?" Bisa asked.

"I demand to see my attorney," blurted Mr. Lambchop.

Bisa looked confused. Then she burst into laughter. "Nobody is going to arrest you, Mr. Lambchop," she said. "You misunderstand. My father is a pilot for the police force!"

3

Emergency!

"SEE THAT MOUNTAIN OVER THERE?" Bisa's father, Captain Tony, was yelling in order to make himself heard over the roar of the tiny airplane's propellers. He gestured out the window. "THAT IS MOUNT KILIMANJARO, THE TALLEST PEAK IN AFRICA."

Stanley and Arthur craned their necks. On the horizon was a majestic white-capped mountain—but instead of rising to a point, it was flat on top.

"It looks like a volcano!" said Arthur.

Captain Tony nodded from behind his sunglasses. "THAT IS BECAUSE IT IS ONE." He laughed. "DO NOT WORRY. IT HAS NOT ERUPTED IN THOUSANDS OF YEARS."

Stanley reached over and shook his father, whose eyes had been squeezed tightly shut since the moment they'd left the ground.

"Dad, you have to see this!"

"No, thank you," croaked Mr. Lambchop. Captain Tony turned the steering column, and the airplane banked hard to the left. Mr. Lambchop pulled his chin down to his chest and grimaced. He did not look well.

Stanley and Arthur grinned at each other.

"NOW LOOK OVER THERE," said Captain Tony.

Stanley looked out the other window, and saw in the distance what appeared to be a giant mirror on the ground. It sparkled in the sun.

"THAT IS LAKE VICTORIA, ONE OF THE LARGEST LAKES ON EARTH. IT IS AS BIG AS NORTH DAKOTA."

"Wow," said Arthur.

The airplane made its way south.

In the bright sun, Stanley could look out his window and see the airplane's shadow following them on the ground below, bounding along like a graceful animal.

Stanley liked to travel. He thought of Mount Rushmore and of Calamity Jane, the adventurous cowgirl they had met there; and of Egypt and Amisi, the archaeologist's daughter; and of Japan and Oda Nobu, the movie star; and of Carmen del Junco, the great matador of Mexico.

He never would have gone to any of those places or met any of those people if he hadn't been flat.

Down below, a giraffe was now running alongside the airplane's shadow. Even from this high up, it was an unusual-looking animal. It had such a very long neck and very thin legs. Stanley had once read that other animals liked to have a giraffe around, because its height allowed it to spot predators sooner. When a giraffe ran, all the animals ran. It was as if having a giraffe nearby helped everyone see farther.

As they crossed the border into Tanzania, the cockpit radio crackled to life. A voice spoke rapidly in Swahili. Captain Tony shouted something back.

"What is it?" asked Arthur.

"THERE IS A BRUSHFIRE IN NAIROBI NATIONAL PARK," said Captain Tony. "THIS PARK IS VERY CLOSE TO OUR CITY. I MUST RETURN AT ONCE."

Mr. Lambchop opened his eyes. "You should land here and let us off," he said bravely.

Captain Tony shook his head. "NO TIME," he said. "YOU WILL HAVE TO JUMP."

Mr. Lambchop's mouth fell open.

Captain Tony commanded Arthur to open a compartment on one side of the plane. Arthur reached inside and then held up a pack in each hand.

"Two parachutes!" he announced.

"THAT IS WHAT I WAS AFRAID OF," said Captain Tony.

"Are these are all there is?" said Mr. Lambchop.

Arthur said, "I think you mean 'Are these all there *are*,' Dad. Grammatically—"

"Quiet, Arthur!" said Mr. Lambchop.

Stanley swallowed. "You two use them," he said. "I can jump without a parachute."

"Stanley Lambchop, you will do no such thing," said Mr. Lambchop. "You may be flat, but you are not a bird."

"Dad, it's the only way," Stanley pleaded. "If I could ride the wind in Canada to the Northwest Territories, then I can be my own parachute."

Mr. Lambchop looked hard at Stanley.

"PLEASE HURRY," Captain Tony said.

Mr. Lambchop blinked. "Don't tell your mother," he said, grabbing a parachute from Arthur.

With Arthur and Mr. Lambchop suited up, they pulled open the cargo door.

Stanley's father hugged him. "Fly safely, son."

Arthur pulled a pair of goggles down over his eyes. He looked out the open door and grinned. "Now this is an adventure!"

And with that, Arthur Lambchop jumped out of the airplane.

"Arthur!" Mr. Lambchop was stunned. "Come back here!" He hurled himself out of the cargo door after his younger son.

Only Stanley remained.

"FOLLOW THE SUN UNTIL YOU COME TO A RIVER," said Captain Tony. "THE PLACE YOU ARE LOOKING FOR IS JUST A FEW

HOURS DOWNSTREAM."

"Thank you," said Stanley. "Good luck with your fire."

"AND GOOD LUCK WITH YOUR SKULL," replied Captain Tony with a salute.

Stanley stepped up to the opening. As he grabbed the handle beside the cargo door, the wind blew his feet out from beneath him. Arthur and his father looked like starfish falling through the air below.

Stanley took three deep breaths.

And then he let go.

On Safari

Instead of falling, Stanley shot upward. He struggled to make his body like a skydiver's, parallel to the earth. But when he did, the wind only lifted him higher, like a piece of paper in a breeze. He was too flat.

Stanley could see the bloomlike parachutes of Arthur and his father far below. I have to get closer, he thought.

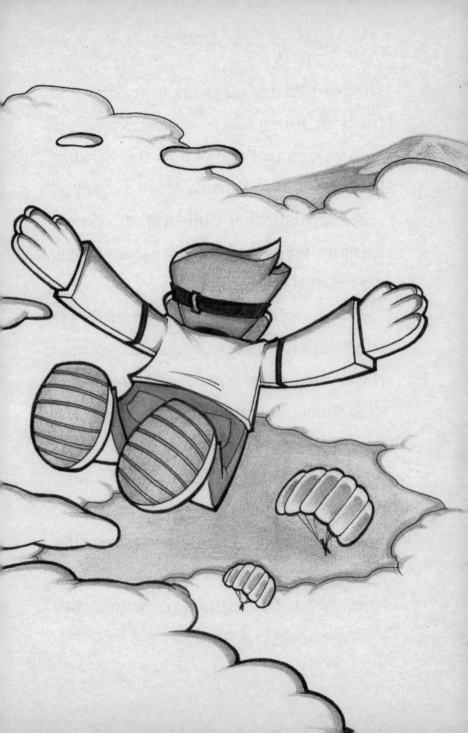

He pointed his arms downward, and his body followed.

Stanley's feet flapped in the wind as he dived down. Within seconds, he had reached his father and brother, slowly descending in their parachutes. He waved at them excitedly.

Mr. Lambchop's eyes widened. He shook his head frantically and pointed toward the ground.

Stanley looked down and saw the yellow land zooming up at him. He was way too low and falling fast. He had to slow down!

With all his might, Stanley bent over and grabbed his feet with his hands, to make his body into a parachute. But instead of catching the wind, he lost control. His body flipped this way and that, blown in wild spirals toward the ground.

Stanley couldn't stop. He was going to crash!

The blades of tall grasses rushed up at him.

Stanley covered his head with his hands as he slammed to the earth.

● ● ●

Stanley coughed amid a cloud of dust and felt the ground with his hands. He couldn't move his legs.

As the dust settled, he saw what had happened. He had crashed feet first into the soft earth, his legs plunging deep into the soil. He pushed the ground with his hands, and his lower body slid out like toothpicks stuck in a sandwich.

He bent his back, flexed his arms, and wriggled his toes. Everything seemed to be in working order. Stanley jumped to his feet. Boy, was he lucky! Being flat had saved his—

The grasses directly to Stanley's right rustled. Then he heard a low growl, and a tuft of brown fur poked out from between them.

A lion was staring right at Stanley!

Stanley held his breath. In school, he had learned how animals protected themselves from predators by blending in with their surroundings.

Maybe if the lion sees only my side, Stanley thought, I'll just look like another blade of grass.

The lion slowly circled in front of him. Stanley inched his narrow side around to face it.

The lion stared and stared. It stared some more.

It shook its head. Then it turned around and disappeared back into the bush.

Stanley allowed himself to breathe at last. It had worked! For the second time in as many minutes, being flat had saved his life!

"Stanley!" His father came plunging through the grass, with Arthur close behind. Mr. Lambchop lifted Stanley in the air and swung him around, Stanley's legs flying.

"I told you he'd be all right." Arthur grinned.

"My goodness!" Mr. Lambchop hugged Stanley tightly. "I was worried!"

"I'm okay," said Stanley. "A lion almost ate me, but I tricked him."

"What?!" said Arthur and Mr. Lambchop.

Stanley told them all about what had happened since he'd jumped out of the plane.

As Stanley finished his story, a herd of zebras appeared nearby, their heads visible above the grasses.

"Hey, Stanley," Arthur said, raising an eyebrow. "Want to play camouflage some more? Because I have an idea."

Arthur told Stanley and their father to collect the tallest blades of grass they could find. Then he attached them to his parachute and helped Stanley drape the whole thing over his shoulders.

When Stanley held out his arms like a bat, he looked just like a long stretch of grass. Arthur showed Mr. Lambchop where to make some holes with his pocketknife.

"We're ready," said Arthur, surveying their work. He and their father gathered behind Stanley and peeked out through the eyeholes. Together, they crept toward the zebras.

The animals' black-and-white stripes blended into one another. Stanley almost couldn't tell where one zebra ended and another began.

"Awesome," whispered Arthur. A few of the zebras swung their heads in the direction of his voice. Their mouths munched grass intently.

Stanley had always wanted to go on a safari, and he couldn't imagine one better than this. The sun was golden. They saw two leopards fighting. They spied a baboon eating insects. They stumbled upon a herd of wildebeests sunning themselves.

And then an elephant walked right in front of them!

"Stanley?" Arthur said in a soft voice.

"Yeah?" said Stanley out of the corner of his mouth. The elephant's feet were the size of pizzas.

"Maybe while we're here, I can get that elephant to flatten me, too."

Stanley strained not to giggle.

"Well, if you boys are both going to be flat," Mr. Lambchop whispered, putting his hand on Stanley's shoulder, "then I suppose I'll have to try it, too."

As the elephant raised its trunk to let out a trumpetlike roar, Stanley could not have felt happier.

5

Down the River

The Lambchops followed the sun westward across the savannah, as Captain Tony had instructed. Soon, more and more trees sprung up around them, and they came to a river. They walked along the muddy bank.

The sun was high in the sky. Drops of sweat ran from Stanley's forehead down his body.

"Are we there yet?" Arthur asked for what seemed like the millionth time.

"No, Arthur," Mr. Lambchop said in a weary voice.

They kept walking. Their shoes made sucking sounds as they stepped in and out of the mud.

Suddenly, there was a low growling, and Stanley froze in fear.

Arthur looked at his stomach. "I'm hungry," he whined.

"Look at that," said Mr. Lambchop, pointing down the bank.

It was a canoe pulled up on the shore.

The Lambchops found a paddle inside. Mr. Lambchop scanned the area.

"Stanley, exactly how far downriver

did Captain Tony say to go?" Mr. Lambchop asked.

"A few hours," replied Stanley.

"On foot? Or by boat?"

Stanley realized he didn't know.

"My feet hurt," grumbled Arthur. "And I have mud in my socks."

"Whose canoe do you think this is?" Stanley asked his father.

Mr. Lambchop shrugged. "I don't know. Perhaps the owners went hunting."

Meanwhile, Arthur climbed into the canoe. "Ahhhh," he said, putting his feet up on a seat.

"Arthur Lambchop," Mr. Lambchop said sternly, "are you stealing someone else's canoe?"

"No." Arthur rolled his eyes. "I'm *sitting* in someone else's canoe."

"Would it be stealing if we borrowed it and brought it right back?" Stanley suggested.

Mr. Lambchop looked at Stanley. "Yes, it would," he said.

There was a rustling in the brush nearby. Onto the bank stepped a very tall man with enormous holes in his earlobes. His body was draped in red cloth, and in his hand was a staff taller than Stanley. He stopped short when he saw the Lambchops.

"Arthur!" Mr. Lambchop whispered out of the side of his mouth.

Arthur nearly jumped out of his skin when he saw the tribesman.

Behind the man, a woman also swathed in red appeared. She held a baby wrapped in patterned cloth close to her body.

The man squinted at the Lambchops. Then he turned and fixed his gaze on Stanley. He came closer. Stanley flinched as the man leaned close and peered behind Stanley's head.

He looked Stanley right in the eye. "What happened to you?" the man asked.

"I was flattened by my own bulletin board," Stanley answered.

"You speak English!" sputtered Mr. Lambchop.

"And French, too," the man said. "I am of the Masai tribe, but I am also a graduate of the Sorbonne in Paris. This land is our home. And you, young man," he continued, turning to Arthur, "what do you think you are doing in our canoe?"

"Don't be so hard on him," the woman said. "He is just a boy. They are clearly lost."

The baby squealed with delight at the sight of Stanley.

Mr. Lambchop rummaged through his pocket and came up with the newspaper clipping. "We're trying to get to the spot marked by the X."

The man and woman studied the article.

"Many believe that the first people lived in Africa," said the man, "and then walked onto the other continents long, long ago when all the parts of the world were close together and had not yet drifted apart. Today, many people come seeking the place they began." He turned to Stanley. "Is this why you have come?"

"I guess so," said Stanley.

The man turned to Mr. Lambchop. "This is only a few hours downriver. Would you like to borrow our canoe?"

"That would be very generous!" said Mr. Lambchop. "Thank you!"

Stanley, Arthur, and Mr. Lambchop waved good-bye to the family as they pulled away from the shore. Soon, they were in the center of the river. A hippopotamus eyed them suspiciously, with only the top of its head and its enormous nostrils visible above the surface.

Stanley and Arthur had both wanted to paddle, and finally Mr. Lambchop agreed to let Stanley have the first turn.

Canoeing was much harder than Stanley expected. The canoe kept drifting toward the shore—"Straighten out, Stanley!" Arthur complained— and then Stanley had to work extra hard

just to keep the boat facing forward.

"Let me try," Arthur snapped.

"I just started," said Stanley.

"Well," said Arthur, "now it's time to finish!"

"No," said Stanley.

"Boys," groaned Mr. Lambchop.

"He's taking forever!" complained Arthur, grabbing the top of the paddle.

"Stop it, Arthur!" said Stanley, pulling back.

"Let me have it!"

"No!"

"Stanley, it's my TURN!" Arthur pulled, and Stanley pulled, and the paddle flew from their hands and flipped into the water with a plop.

"The paddle!" gasped Mr. Lambchop. He reached over the side of the canoe and started splashing with his hands, trying to reach it.

"It was HIS fault!" Arthur and Stanley yelled at each other.

"I don't care whose fault it was!" shouted Mr. Lambchop. "Get that paddle!"

Arthur and Stanley plunged their hands into the water and tried to get the boat to move closer to the paddle. But it was too late. The current was carrying it down the river.

As the canoe drifted aimlessly, Mr. Lambchop put his head in his hands.

Stanley and Arthur both stared at

their feet.

Finally, Mr. Lambchop looked at his watch, shook his head, and sighed. "Your mother is at her Grammar Society fund-raiser right now. I'm sure she and her fellow grammarians would appreciate our predicament."

Stanley and Arthur exchanged curious glances.

"Today, we have discovered the origin of a common expression in the English language. We are, as they say, up a creek without a paddle."

Mr. Lambchop's lips curled into a smile. Stanley and Arthur started to giggle.

When their laughter died down, Mr.

Lambchop looked at them earnestly. "I expect the two of you to pay for that paddle out of your allowance," he said. "We gave that family our word that we would return their canoe as we found it. Do you understand?"

"Yes," said Stanley and Arthur.

"We are Lambchop men in deepest Africa," said Mr. Lambchop. "We must work together."

A minute later, Stanley's shoes and socks lay on the floor of the canoe. With one hand on Stanley's head and another on his leg, his father pulled Stanley's legs through the water. Using Stanley as their paddle, the Lambchops made their way downriver.

6

Dr. Livingston Fallows

As night fell, Mr. Lambchop admitted that he could paddle no more. Stanley was too heavy. Their journey downriver was supposed to take only a few hours, but as far as Stanley could tell they were still a long way from their destination.

As strange birds chirped and mysterious splashes occasionally erupted in the darkness around them,

Stanley huddled in the bottom of the boat with Arthur. Their father squeezed in beside them.

Exhausted, the Lambchop men fell asleep in a heap, their canoe adrift. The African river had defeated them.

"Hallo!" Stanley was awakened by a voice. It was a man standing on the shore, wearing high boots, khaki pants, and a brown shirt. He had a British accent. "You there! Are you all right?"

"Oh, thank goodness," Mr. Lambchop said under his breath.

Stanley sunk his arms in the water at the back of the canoe and flicked his wrists up and down. The boat made its way slowly toward the shore.

"We are looking for an archaeological site!" called Mr. Lambchop. "Can you help us?"

The man shaded his eyes. He walked several steps into the water and jumped back.

"I say! Does that boy have a flat head?" he cried as the canoe lifted onto shore.

"Hello," said Stanley, drying his hands on his pants. "I'm Stanley."

The man's eyes bulged. Without another word, he turned and ran into the jungle.

"Hey!" cried Arthur. "Come back!"

"Perhaps he's going to get us a towel,"

said Mr. Lambchop.

Stanley, Arthur, and Mr. Lambchop followed a well-worn path away from the water. Soon, they came to a clearing dotted with canvas tents.

Out of the largest tent charged a very large man with a very large white mustache. Behind him shuffled the man from the shore, who appeared to be his assistant.

The large man stopped short at the sight of Stanley. He held up his hand, and his assistant walked right into it with a slap. "I'll handle this," the man with the mustache boomed.

Several people emerged from other tents, including a woman clutching a camera. They gathered around curiously.

The man marched up to Stanley. Without a word of greeting, he pulled out a ruler and measured the thickness of Stanley's head. Then he carefully rapped him on the crown in four different spots, appearing to

listen carefully each time. He gestured
gruffly for Stanley to open his mouth.
He peered inside. Finally, he tugged
Stanley's ear.

"Ouch," said Stanley.

"Harrumph," the man grumbled.
He turned to his audience. "I hereby
pronounce this scoundrel a fraud!"

The woman with the camera snapped
a picture.

"I beg your pardon?" said Stanley's father.

"Don't be fooled," the man said. "This boy is NOT a genuine, living, flat Homo sapiens."

"I am, too," protested Stanley.

"He totally is," agreed Arthur. "You should see him rolled up."

Mr. Lambchop was red. "Who do you think you are?" he asked the man sharply.

"I, sir, am Dr. Livingston Fallows, the world's greatest ologist!"

"What's an ologist?" said Arthur.

"It's everything," the man answered proudly. "Anthropologist, paleontologist,

72

archaeologist, et cetera."

"Well," said Mr. Lambchop, "my sons and I have traveled all the way from the United States of America in order to see a flat skull that has been discovered by *real* scientists in this area. And I think we'd prefer not to spend another moment with a *fraud* like you."

The man huffed with indignity. He pointed an enormous finger in Mr. Lambchop's face. "You wouldn't say that if you saw the skull!"

The crowd around them murmured.

Stanley's heart skipped a beat. "You mean it's here?" he said. "The flat skull is here?"

They had made it, at last.

"Please, Dr. Fallows, sir." Stanley's voice was shaking. "May I see the skull?"

7

The Flat Skull

"I present to you," thundered Dr. Fallows in the dim light of his tent, "the flat skull of Rufiji!"

Stanley, Arthur, and Mr. Lambchop all gasped.

The skull was flattened the wrong way!

Instead of being flat the way Stanley was flat—front and back—its edge was

down the middle. Dr. Fallows turned the skull sideways, and Stanley could see right in one eye socket and out the other.

Nobody spoke for a long while.

Arthur shook his head. "Look at its teeth," he said almost to himself. Stanley saw that they were very small and jagged.

"That's not a person," Arthur said suddenly.

"Not anymore!" beamed Dr. Fallows.

"It's a big fish!"

At once, Stanley could see that his brother was right.

Dr. Fallows rotated the skull in his hand. Something changed in his eyes,

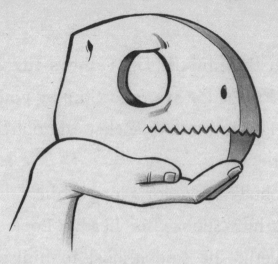

and he swung around to his assistant.
"You fool!" he cried. "Of course this is a
fish! How dare you suggest otherwise!"
With a grunt, he flung the skull out of
the tent.

Stanley's eyes welled up with tears,
and he ran from the scene.

"Stanley!"

Mr. Lambchop and Arthur found
Stanley where he had folded himself at

the edge of the jungle. "Stanley, what's wrong?"

Arthur kneeled down. "What is it, Stanley?"

Finally, Stanley lifted his wet face and wiped it with the back of his hands.

"It's just that . . ." He let out a heavy sigh. "We came all this way, and . . . I didn't find out anything about . . . about why I'm flat." His voice broke, and his face crinkled into a sob.

"Stanley." His father squeezed his shoulder. "Don't you see? These last few days have been the most remarkable of my entire life."

"It's the best vacation ever," said Arthur.

"What a time we've had! We jumped from a plane and went on a safari. We met Masai tribesmen and canoed through deepest Africa. And it's all because of you."

A smile crept across Stanley's face. "We *have* had a lot of fun," he admitted.

"I wouldn't trade any of it," said Mr. Lambchop. "Except maybe for a new paddle."

Stanley chuckled as his father and brother wrapped him in a hug.

"We're glad you're flat, Stanley," Arthur said.

Surrounded by his family, Stanley thought of the long-necked giraffe on the plains, surrounded by all the other animals. They liked having him around. He helped them to see farther.

8

A Souvenir

At the airport in America, Harriet Lambchop shrieked with excitement when Stanley, Arthur, and their father came through the door at ARRIVALS. She ran up and threw her arms around Stanley.

"How I missed you!" she cried. She squeezed Stanley's edges. "You've lost weight!"

"How's my little explorer?" She ruffled Arthur's hair.

"We saw an elephant!" said Arthur.

Then she spun and gazed into Mr. Lambchops eyes. They kissed deeply.

"Ew," said Arthur. "We're in *public*."

Harriett said, "Wait until you see what I got for you!" She pulled two large, oddly shaped pillows out of shopping bags. She handed one to Arthur and one to Stanley.

The pillows looked like curved raindrops.

"What is it?" said Arthur.

"I won them in the silent auction at the Grammar Society fund-raiser! That," she said, pointing to Arthur's, "is a crocheted comma. And yours, Stanley, is a single quotation mark!"

"What's the difference?" asked Arthur.

Mrs. Lambchop blinked. "Proper usage, of course!"

Back at home, Stanley stood in front of his enormous bulletin board. It was dotted with souvenirs from his travels: a postcard from Calamity Jasper, a newspaper clipping from Canada, and photographs from Mexico and Japan. In his hands, he held the newspaper article that the Lambchops had carried with them on their African adventure: FLAT SKULL DISCOVERED IN AFRICA.

It was crumpled and torn in several places, stained by water and mud, but it was still in one piece.

Stanley pinned it carefully to the bulletin board.

Arthur's hand appeared beside Stanley's. Arthur fiddled with a pushpin just above the newspaper article. Then he hung something on it.

It was the flat skull of Rufiji!

Stanley gasped. "How did— Where did you—"

"It was lying on the ground outside Dr. Fallows's tent after you ran off." Arthur grinned. "I figured you might want it—you know, to remind you who you really are."

Stanley's stomach fluttered as the skull swung gently on its pushpin. Then he noticed that Arthur had the comma pillow strapped to his back like a mane, and the quotation mark pillow curving up over his head. He'd pinned spots of dark fabric all over.

Arthur was a giraffe! He swept a blanket off his bed and held it out to Stanley. "Want to go on a safari in the laundry room?"

"Absolutely!" said Stanley. And together, the Lambchop boys headed off on another adventure.

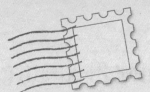

WHAT YOU NEED TO KNOW
TO GO ON YOUR OWN
AFRICAN SAFARI

Four of the five fastest land animals on
Earth live in Africa: cheetahs, wildebeest,
lions, and Thomson's gazelle.

Africa is the second-largest of the
Earth's continents. It covers 11,699,000
square miles and makes up about 22 percent
of the world's land area. With over 50
countries, Africa has more than
any other continent.

Giraffes are about 2 meters (6 feet) tall when they are born. Their tongues can be so long—up to 18 inches—that they can reach their ears with them!

While many have tried, zebras have never been successfully domesticated like horses.

Elephants can weigh up to 6 or 7 tons and have no natural enemies in the animal kingdom. They're not predators and there are no other animals large enough to challenge them.

The Namib desert is the oldest in the world, and the only desert in Africa inhabited by giraffes, lions, elephants, and rhino.

Africa is almost an island. Its only connection to other land is the tiny Sinai Peninsula in Egypt!

Take a sneak peek at

The Flying Chinese
Wonders

The fact that Stanley Lambchop was flat did not mean he enjoyed being treated like a poster.

Stanley trudged back and forth outside the school auditorium with a giant piece of cardboard taped to the front of his body. It read:

THE FLYING CHINESE WONDERS

A CHINESE NEW YEAR PERFORMANCE

FOR THE WHOLE COMMUNITY

People streamed inside. A beefy boy from Stanley's class called out, "Look, it's the poster boy for flat kids!"

Stanley grimaced. He hoped no one else would notice him.

"Well, hello there, Stanley Lambchop!" It was Doctor Dan, whom Stanley had visited just after he was flattened. It wasn't long ago that he'd woken up to find that his bulletin board had fallen on him in the middle of the night. "Helping out with the big performance, are we? Well, good for you for making positive use of an unusual condition!"

How embarrassing, Stanley thought.

After Doctor Dan left to take his seat, Stanley's family appeared. "My little star!" squealed his mother, Harriet Lambchop.

Stanley tried to smile as she kissed the edge of his head.

His little brother, Arthur, rolled his eyes. "He's not even *in the show,* Mom."

"Now, Arthur," Mrs. Lambchop said, "those behind the scenes are just as important as those onstage."

"And nobody is behind the scenes like our Stanley." Mr. Lambchop winked. Stanley sighed. He'd always liked being in plays. Now, all anyone wanted him to do was move the sets, because his shape made him hard to see when he crossed the stage.

"I'm not even moving scenery today," Stanley grumbled.

"Why not?" asked Mr. Lambchop.

"Are you in charge of the giant pandas?" said Mrs. Lambchop hopefully. "They have always been my favorite wonders from China!"

"No." Stanley pouted. "There aren't any pandas. The spotlight blew a fuse, so . . ," He held up a giant flashlight from behind his poster. "I have to hang upside down from the ceiling with this."

"Hey, Stanley," called his friend

Carlos, who lived next door to the Lambchops. "Don't break a leg!"

Stanley's mother chuckled. "He means, 'Break a leg,' dear. That's a common figure of speech in the theater. It means good luck!" Harriet Lambchop took great interest in the proper use of the English language.

"I don't think so, Mom," said Arthur. "I think Carlos meant, 'Don't fall from the ceiling and break your leg.'"

"Be quiet, Arthur," huffed Stanley.

Once everyone was seated, Stanley took his place. He hung with his lower body rolled around a bar high over the crowd.

It's not fair! he thought. Why do I have to save the day any time somebody needs something flat or flexible?

On the one hand, Stanley's new shape allowed him to do lots of fun and exciting things, like fit between the walls of an Egyptian pyramid and be a cape in a Mexican bullfight. On the other hand, he was often asked to do uncomfortable, humiliating, and boring things that would never be expected of a rounded person. For instance, he had been rolled and tied to the back of a horse in South Dakota and on another trip he had been forced to ride with baggage in the cargo hold of an airplane to Africa.

Stanley didn't want to hang high in the air holding a heavy flashlight. He didn't even know what to expect onstage. The performers had arrived only moments before the show was about to begin.

The lights went down. With a sigh, Stanley lifted his flashlight and flicked it on as the curtains squeaked open.

In the center of the bare stage stood a teenage boy and girl. They wore matching red outfits.

"Lucky people of America!" A Chinese man in a tuxedo stepped onto the stage. "All the way from the People's Republic of China, we bring to you . . . the Flying Chinese Wonders!"

A few people clapped as Stanley moved his spotlight back and forth between the two performers. They bowed slowly.

This is going to be even worse than I thought, figured Stanley.

Then, in a flash, the boy and girl shot into the air. Flipping high over the stage, they grabbed hands and flattened their bodies, spinning around each other like a sputtering propeller headed straight for the ground. Stanley held his breath as the human propeller spun faster and faster, its descent slowing until finally it hovered a few feet off the ground. They planted their feet and faced the audience with their arms raised in the air. The entire auditorium erupted with applause.

Stanley couldn't believe it! The Flying Chinese Wonders were amazing! They swooped and sailed through the air. They twisted and flipped and spun like tops. Together, they became a dragon, a comet, and a fish on a trampoline. Sometimes, Stanley could not tell where the first Wonder began and the other ended.

Their bodies can do anything! Stanley thought. His flashlight raced to keep up.

For their grand finale, the Flying Chinese Wonders connected head to toe, puffed out their chests to form a circle, and rolled around the stage. When they came to a stop, each held out an arm and a leg. The giant circle had become the sun.

It was the greatest thing Stanley had ever seen! He shouted, whooped, and clapped his—

Stanley's heart plummeted as he watched the giant flashlight drop from his hands.

CRAAASH!

The Flying Chinese Wonders looked up in alarm. Their circle shook . . . and collapsed to the floor in a heap.